Inspiring Collective Biographies

PIONEERING AMERICAN COMPUTER GENIUSES

Mary Northrup

Enslow Publishers, Inc.
40 Industrial Road
Box 398
Berkeley Heights, NJ 07922
USA
http://www.enslow.com

Original edition published as *American Computer Pioneers* in 1998.

Library of Congress Cataloging-in-Publication Data

Northrup, Mary.
[American computer pioneers]
Pioneering American computer geniuses / Mary Northrup.
pages cm
Includes bibliographical references and index.
Summary: "Read about these American computer geniuses including Herman Hollerith, John von Neumann, Grace Hopper, John W. Mauchly and J. Presper Eckert, Jr, An Wang, Jack Kilby and Robert Noyce, Bill Gates, Steven Jobs and Stephen Wozniak, Marc Hannah and Marc Andreessen"— Provided by publisher.
ISBN 978-0-7660-4167-7
1. Computer scientists—United States Biography —uvenile literature. 2. Inventors—United States—Biography--Juvenile literature. 3. Computers—History—Juvenile literature. I. Title.
QA76.17.N68 2013
004.092'2—dc23
[B]

2012024625

Future editions:
Paperback ISBN: 978-1-4644-0273-9 EPUB ISBN: 978-1-4645-1173-8
Single-User PDF ISBN: 978-1-4646-1173-5 Multi-User PDF ISBN: 978-0-7660-5802-6

Printed in the United States of America.

042013 Lake Book Manufacturing, Inc., Melrose Park, IL

10 9 8 7 6 5 4 3 2 1

To Our Readers: We have done our best to make sure all Internet addresses in this book were active and appropriate when we went to press. However, the author and the publisher have no control over and assume no liability for the material available on those Internet sites or on other Web sites they may link to. Any comments or suggestions can be sent by e-mail to comments@enslow.com or to the address on the back cover.

♻ Enslow Publishers, Inc., is committed to printing our books on recycled paper. The paper in every book contains 10% to 30% post-consumer waste (PCW). The cover board on the outside of each book contains 100% PCW. Our goal is to do our part to help young people and the environment too!

Photo Credits: AP Images/Tammie Arroyo, p. 88; ©Bettman/Corbis/AP Images, p. 50; ©I. Inoue/AP Images, p. 54; Anthony Hall / Shutterstock.com, p.79; AP Images, p. 36; Apple Computer, Inc, p. 73; Intel Corporation, p. 60; Lakeside School, p. 70; Library of Congress, pp. 8, 24; Los Alamos National Laboratory, p. 18; Netscape Communications Corporation, pp. 92, 98; Silicon Graphics, Inc., pp. 83; The estate of Dr. An Wang and the Trustees of The Wang Foundation, p. 45; U.S. Army, p. 42; U.S. Census Bureau, p. 14; U.S. Navy, p. 26; Unisys Corporation, p. 32; Used with permission from Microsoft, p. 63

Cover Photo: Used with permission from Microsoft

Contents

Preface

Computer technology is one of the greatest developments of the twentieth century. Like most other complex machines, the computer was not invented in one day by one person. It evolved through the work of many people. Some built the hardware. Others were master programmers. Some were "idea people"—brilliant at theories. And some were hands-on business experts.

American computer pioneers are a special band. With a vision of the future, they transformed the world. Calculations that once took days with a pencil and paper now take seconds. Whole libraries fit on a CD-ROM, and one thumb-sized flash drive can hold hundreds of feature-length films. Dangerous jobs that used to be done by workers are now done by robots. Mind-numbing records are processed and kept in a computer's memory rather than written by hand and warehoused in boxes.

Who are these people who so radically changed the way life is lived? They come from a wide variety of backgrounds and working styles. Some were friendly and outgoing; others were shy and reserved. Their families were wealthy or working class. A few had parents who were engineers or scientists. Many of these people took a new path.

Some worked alone; others, with partners. In most partnerships, each person took over the area in which he or she was expert. An example of a good partnership: Steve Jobs and Steve Wozniak. Although both were "techies," Wozniak was the computer builder; Jobs, the company builder.

Most computer pioneers liked science or math when they were young. Many were into the electronic gadgets of their time. All were smart, creative, determined, and focused. They concentrated on their jobs or their ideas completely and for long stretches of time. Sleeping at the lab or office was common during big projects. They kept at it until a breakthrough came. For them, it was not only work but also fun. They enjoyed solving problems.

In the early days of computing, these pioneers were concentrated in the eastern cities. In Washington, D.C., the center of the nation's government, Herman Hollerith invented his tabulating machine. John von Neumann put his magnificent brain to work at the Institute for Advanced Study in Princeton, New Jersey. At Harvard University near Boston, Grace Hopper programmed some of the first computers. An Wang started his company in South Boston. John W. Mauchly and J. Presper Eckert, Jr., built UNIVAC in Pennsylvania.

Bridging the big computers and the microprocessors, Jack Kilby and Robert Noyce invented the "chip." Kilby did this between the two coasts—in Texas. Noyce, already in California, was among the first on the West Coast to catch the next computing wave.

Bill Gates based his company, Microsoft, in Washington State. Steve Jobs and Steve Wozniak made California the home of Apple Computer, Inc. California also attracted Marc Hannah and Marc Andreessen from the Midwest. Hannah cofounded Silicon Graphics, Inc., and Andreessen wrote the program for what would become Netscape® Navigator.

A journalist named their part of California "Silicon Valley," for the silicon chips used in computers. Located southeast of San Francisco, Silicon Valley is world famous for its computer companies.

By far the most impressive change in computers has been their size. The computers on which von Neumann, Hopper, Mauchly, and Eckert worked were room-size. For all their bulk, they were slow. These machines were used only by government and big businesses. A home computer was still science fiction.

Once Kilby and Noyce invented the microchip, the technology existed to build a handheld computer. Speed increased, and size decreased even more. The personal computer (PC) became a reality. The trend continued, making way for laptops, tablet computers, and smartphones that are capable of recording videos and browsing the Internet as well as making calls.

These changes opened the way for thousands of inventors to imagine new uses and products for computers. These inventions brought a world of change in how people accomplish tasks both large and small—exploring space, building cars, publishing news, controlling traffic lights, cooking meals, listening to music, shopping, paying bills, sending messages, or playing games. From the largest company to the smallest individual, computer technology has changed lives.

American computer pioneers made it possible.

Herman Hollerith

1

Herman Hollerith

Processing Data With Punched Cards

For Herman Hollerith, a train ride changed his ideas about handling data. He watched the conductor punch tickets. To make the ticket valid, the conductor added a description of the passenger. When the hair color, eye color, and so on were punched on the ticket, it showed a "punch photograph." Hollerith would one day punch holes in cards to speed the count of people in the census.

Hollerith was an engineer and inventor. During his lifetime, he patented many devices. Maybe the background of his family helped. Some of them were skilled locksmiths. Others designed and made horse-drawn carriages. Johann and Franciska, his parents, were German immigrants. They settled in Buffalo, New York, where Herman was born on February 29, 1860.

When Hollerith was just seven years old, his father died. His mother was left with five children to support. She quickly turned her hat-making skills into a business.

The future inventor disliked spelling. Once he even jumped out a school window to escape a spelling lesson.[1] When he was fifteen, he was already at the College of the City of New York. From there, he went to Columbia School of Mines in New York City, where he did well in engineering and math. He also excelled in drawing. His way of seeing things and his precise memory led to his talent for invention.[2]

After graduation from Columbia in 1879, Hollerith was hired by the Census Office in Washington, D.C. Workers with good math backgrounds were needed.

At work Herman Hollerith met John Shaw Billings. Dr. Billings was in charge of vital statistics (numbers of births and deaths). When Billings took the young man home for family meals, the two discussed census problems.

During one of these talks, Billings suggested a machine. He thought a device based on the Jacquard loom might work. This loom, invented in 1801, made complex patterns in cloth using punch cards. The Jacquard loom changed the weaving industry. Hollerith always gave Billings the credit for the idea of the punched card system.[3] Hollerith wanted to make a business of it, so he began work based on the idea.

Counting the population was not easy. First, census workers went to each house with sheets of paper called schedules. On the schedule, they wrote the answers to questions they asked each person: What is your name? Your age? Male or female? Your race? Your work? Where were you born? Were your parents born in another country? Can you read? Did you attend school? Are you a voter? and much more.[4] Then, the answers from all over the country had to be counted. It could take years to finish.

Hollerith designed a machine to count and sort all these answers. He did not use punch cards at first. He used a roll of paper on which each line stood for one person. A hole was punched along that line for age, another for sex, and so on. Then he rolled the paper to the next line for the next person. When a roll was filled, it was fed into a machine. Metal pins in this machine found the holes and touched a metal drum. There an electromagnet was activated. That made a counter go forward by one. After a whole roll was fed through, the data showed—right there on the counters.

Hollerith's idea was good for collecting the numbers. Still he had a problem. To look at any one piece of data, he had to go back through miles of paper.

Remembering his talk with Dr. Billings, and recalling that train conductor, he invented the punched card system. One card would hold one person's census information. The areas for the information lined the outside of the card, because a hand punch (like the conductor's) could only reach a short way. A machine would "read" the holes in the card. The device was not used in the 1880 census. Years of work to perfect it lay ahead.

While he was experimenting, Hollerith taught for a year in Cambridge at the Massachusetts Institute of Technology (MIT). After the school year, he went to work for the United States Patent Office in Washington, D.C. A year later he was in business for himself.

Hollerith wanted to make sure his punched card system worked before the 1890 census. Between 1886 and 1889, he used it to process data for the city of Baltimore, the Health Office of New Jersey, and the Health Department of New York City.

During these test runs, he found out what punching the cards with a hand punch was like. After one thousand a day, his arm ached badly.[5] So he invented a keyboard, or pantograph punch. This machine was much easier on the arm. Hollerith simply pushed a stylus into the model plate on one side, and a hole was punched in the card on the other side. His invention also made reading the cards easier, because the holes were placed exactly.[6]

Hollerith's system, then, had several parts. The punch put the holes in the cards. The card reader, like his early machine, passed pins through the holes. These pins reached mercury cups that made an electrical circuit. Then the card sorter grouped cards with certain categories into compartments. The tabulator kept a count of the number of holes it sensed.

The Census Office tested several systems and decided Hollerith's was the fastest. Clerks fed about eight thousand; cards each day through the machine (one clerk set a record of 19,071!).[7] Once the schedules were brought in, it took only six weeks for the system operators to have a population count. On December 12, 1890, the Census Office announced there were 62,622,250 people in the United States.[8]

Hollerith received much praise for his new system. Other countries—Austria, Canada, France, and Italy—lined up to order. He even traveled to St. Petersburg for the first Russian census.

Yet Hollerith did not like travel.[9] It took him away from his family. On September 15, 1890, he had married Lucia Talcott. It seems to have been a happy match. Lu, quiet and emotionally strong, was adored by her temperamental husband.[10] They had six children: Lucia; Herman, Jr.; Charles; Nan; Richard; and Virginia. Hollerith was an involved father who worried about their health. He did not hesitate to bother their family doctor with many questions.[11]

Along with his family, Hollerith's Tabulating Machine Company was growing. Businesses wanted a Hollerith system for their accounting and inventory work. Some of his first customers were railroads. Later, department stores and large manufacturing companies wanted the system too.

By the end of the century; Hollerith was busy preparing for the 1900 census. He had to process even more information. One punch card for each

Hollerith built his tabulating machine to count the people of the United States in the 1890 census.

person plus one card for each family had to be run through the machines. More agriculture statistics were needed, so a card for each farm and a card for each crop was made. Hollerith invented a key punch to replace the pantograph. He also continued to make changes with the cards. Always on guard against mistakes, he worked hard to make sure his machines' results were correct.[12]

In two and a half years, Hollerith's machines had completed tabulating the 1900 census. By hand, it would have taken almost eight years.[13]

Early in the new century, the Census Office became the Bureau of the Census. The new director wanted to save money. He thought the government should build its own system. Hollerith tried to stop the bureau on grounds of patent infringement. However, he saw a long battle so did not press on. Hollerith was out of the census business.

His many other business accounts ensured that his company continued to grow. As always, his life was his work and family. He found time to build model trains with his sons and to provide scrap paper from the punch cards for his daughters' school.[14] He also experimented with photography, a lifelong hobby.

Hollerith sold the Tabulating Machine Company in 1911. With two other companies, it became the Computing-Tabulating-Recording Company (CTR). With the sale, Hollerith made a lot of money.

Because he had high blood pressure, his doctor warned him to take it easy. Yet after years of work, he could not retire completely. He planned the building of his estate, including a small farm. He entertained friends and neighbors. For travel and leisure, he bought several boats.

Hollerith did not leave CTR altogether. He sat in on meetings and approved design changes. When Thomas Watson took over as general manager in 1914, Hollerith gradually let go. Watson was to lead the company to great heights. In 1924, CTR's name was changed to International Business Machines (IBM). IBM became one of the leading computer companies of the twentieth century.

Hollerith never lost his interest in machines. He was ever the engineer, designing and inventing. Toward the end of his life, he was in poor health but surrounded by a loving family. He died on November 17, 1929, at age sixty-nine.

Hollerith's punched card system was used for decades after he patented it. Because his devices were electromechanical (and not just mechanical), they can be considered the forerunners of today's computers. His work marked the beginning of modern data processing.

2

John von Neumann

Computer Architect

Few people can be called "genius," but John von Neumann certainly can. He was not only a brilliant mathematician but also a pioneer in game theory, physics, and weather science. His design for computers earned them the name "von Neumann machines." He did more than anyone else of his time to convince scientists and the government that computers were important.

John Louis von Neumann was born on December 28, 1903, in Budapest, Hungary. His Hungarian name was Janos, but he was called Jancsi. His parents, Max and Margaret, had two more sons after John: Michael and Nicholas. Because they were well-off, his parents could afford tutors and good schools. They encouraged reading and learning.

John von Neumann

Little Jancsi was a child prodigy. By age six, he was joking with his father in Greek. He could memorize anything. His family entertained guests by having them ask him questions about a page in the phone book that he had just read quickly.[1]

Max kept his son supplied with books. Jancsi especially liked to read history. In fact, he would refuse to get a haircut unless his mother allowed him to take a history book along.[2] When his parents arranged cello lessons for him, they could not understand why he was not progressing. They later found out that he had a math or history book on the music stand; he was reading while his fingers played the scales.[3]

At school, von Neumann did very well in most classes. When the youth showed talent in math, his father hired university mathematicians to coach him. Before von Neumann was eighteen, he published a scientific paper with one of his tutors.

Because he was so far beyond his classmates in knowledge and ability, von Neumann could have been an outcast, but he was not. Although he could best anyone in a discussion, he knew the other person would resent that. So he tried to be friendly. As he grew up, he learned how to tell humorous stories and jokes to put everyone in a good mood.[4]

After high school, von Neumann entered college to study chemical engineering. He received his degree in 1925, but at the same time he was also taking courses for his doctorate in mathematics. In 1926, he received his Ph.D. from the University of Budapest.

His first professional job was teaching math at the University of Berlin. He also did research and published his findings in scientific journals. Throughout the academic world, the name of von Neumann gained fame. He was invited to teach at Princeton University in New Jersey.

Before he left, however, he made a trip home to Budapest. There, he married Mariette Kovesi on January 1, 1930. He had known Mariette since they were young. They took an ocean liner across the Atlantic to the United States. There, Janos became known as John, or Johnny to his friends.

Von Neumann taught at Princeton for three years. He was famous for writing in one corner of a big blackboard, then erasing the numbers before his students could write them in their notebooks.[5] He was also famous for his bad driving. His many accidents at one intersection earned it the nickname "Von Neumann Corner."[6]

In 1933, he became a professor of mathematics at the Institute for Advanced Study in Princeton. For the rest of his life, he stayed with the institute. There, he continued to build his reputation as one of the most brilliant minds in mathematics. The institute also became the home of Albert Einstein at this time.

His photographic memory and calculating speed became legendary around Princeton. He once helped a student with a difficult math question, writing it on the blackboard and explaining the proof. A few days later, the student told von Neumann he had forgotten the proof. Von Neumann repeated it standing where they were—in the middle of a crowded party.[7] He could also figure complicated problems in his head, while others spent hours with a calculator.

And it was not just math that he remembered. When asked how the novel *A Tale of Two Cities* starts, von Neumann stated the famous first line. He then continued with the rest of the first chapter, reciting for about ten minutes.

For all his talents, von Neumann was not a show-off. He liked others to feel at ease around him. He once told a confused student, "Young man, one never really understands mathematics. One just gets used to it."[8]

In 1935, a baby girl was born to von Neumann and his wife. They named her Marina. Two years later, the couple divorced. Von Neumann later married Klara Dan, who was also from Budapest.

In Europe, tension was building. World War II would soon begin. Von Neumann became an American citizen in 1937. Besides his job at the institute, he now worked for the Army's Ballistic Research Laboratory. Later, he would serve on various defense committees and work for the Navy. He saw the vast amount of calculations that were done. By the late 1930s, he knew that some sort of electronic computing was coming.[9]

During the war, he worked with other experts on the Manhattan Project. This top-secret group built the atomic bomb in Los Alamos, New Mexico.

Von Neumann's math and science genius made him essential to the project. Using punch cards and sorters, he solved equations as part of a math model of a bomb explosion. This model proved that the "implosion method" of detonation would work.

Now he knew that machines were needed to calculate quickly and correctly. By accident, von Neumann learned about the first electronic computer. During a train trip on one of his many travels, he met Herman Goldstine. In awe of the great von Neumann, Goldstine introduced himself. He told von Neumann that he worked on the Electronic Numerical Integrator and Computer (ENIAC) that was even then being built by J. Presper Eckert, Jr., and John W. Mauchly.

Von Neumann was allowed to visit the ENIAC project. His interest gave it more prestige among scientists. (There were still some who thought it was a waste of time and money.) Yet von Neumann was fascinated. He was "[l]ike a child with a new toy,"[10] Mauchly later wrote.

The three men consulted about the main problem with ENIAC: It had no memory. They designed Electronic Discrete Variable Automatic Computer (EDVAC), a machine with programmable storage. Here the dispute starts. Von Neumann wrote the *First Draft of a Report on the EDVAC*. His work was "the first written account of the stored-program computer."[11] Goldstine sent copies to scientists who were not connected to the secret ENIAC project. So those outside the project thought that von

Neumann created the stored-program concept. Yet Eckert and Mauchly claimed that they originated the idea. A later court ruling declared that none of them could claim the patent.

Von Neumann also wrote on game theory. As a young boy in Budapest during World War I, he and his brothers played war games on graph paper. As an adult, he envisioned a theory of games: Knowing the other person's strategy is just as important as the odds of winning. Conflict, trust, and distrust could be analyzed, thought von Neumann.[12] Then this theory could be used in economic or social problems.

After World War II, von Neumann was in great demand. Yet he stayed on at the Institute for Advanced Study. There, he led the Electronic Computer Project. The resulting computer was one of the first with program storage. His design influenced all future computers.

A computer with "von Neumann architecture" stores programs. (These programs are stored as data, just as data that are processed are stored.) It works serially—one step or operation at a time. It has input-output devices. Von Neumann machines are used even today. (This book was written on one.)

In the mid–twentieth century, many people were confused about, even scared of, computers. Yet when von Neumann spoke, scientists, government officials, and the public listened. His speeches and writings (and popular articles about him) convinced people.

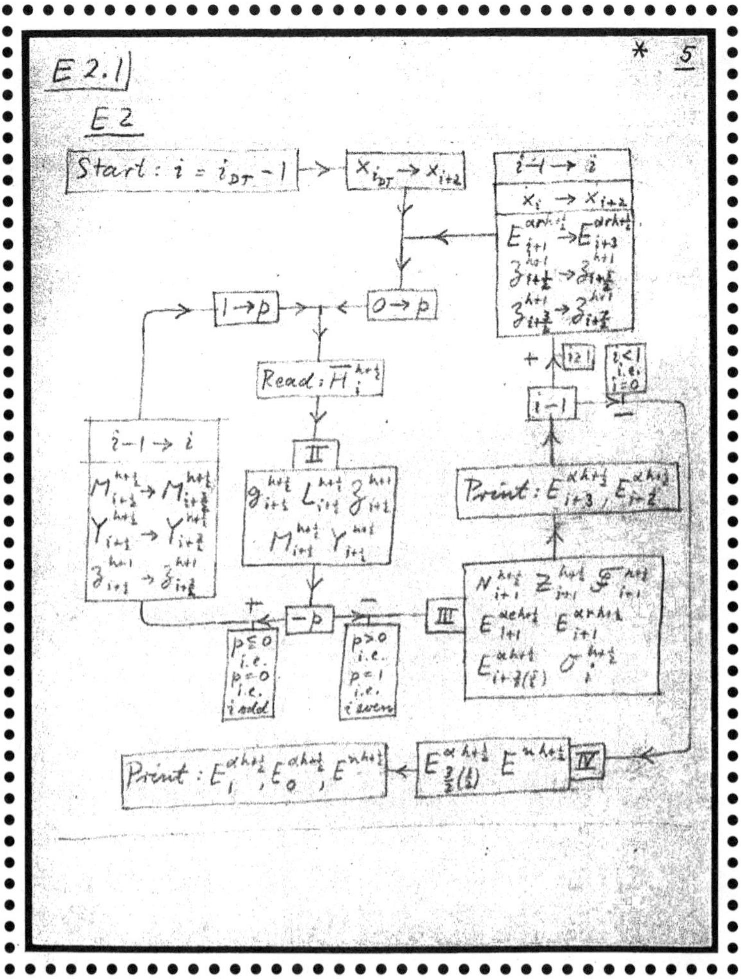

Immediately after World War II, the United States began developing "supercomputers," machines capable of processing massive amounts of information at high speeds. At first developed for military uses, these computers allowed the United States to establish technological dominance in this vital field. Here is a flow diagram, devised in 1950 by John von Neumann for the ENIAC, one of the early American supercomputers.

In 1954, President Dwight D. Eisenhower named von Neumann to the Atomic Energy Commission (AEC). The von Neumanns moved to Washington, D.C. Marina, who had come to live with her father and stepmother during her teen years, went with them.

Von Neumann worked hard at the AEC, just as he had all his life. "His capacity for work was practically unlimited,"[13] remembered his wife. He would often stay up till early morning. His writings eventually filled six large volumes. Still he also knew how to relax. He and Klara were well known for their parties.

All this came to a near-stop in the summer of 1955. Von Neumann fell and hurt his shoulder. When the pain did not lessen, his doctors did some medical tests. They found bone cancer. He continued working, but he gradually weakened. Toward the end of his life, he was in terrible pain. His doctors gave him very strong medication. As a result, all the people who took care of him had to have security clearances. It was feared he might unknowingly give away military secrets.

He died on February 8, 1957. He never lived to see computers in all areas of life. Yet they are everywhere because of his work. He foresaw their potential power and designed machines that would achieve this potential. Von Neumann—scientist, consultant, teacher, promoter—was the genius of computer technology.

Grace Hopper

3

Grace Hopper

Amazing Grace

"There's a bug in the system!" A programmer says this when something goes wrong with a computer. It does not mean an ant or a beetle is crawling around inside. However, the very first computer bug was a real insect. A moth flew into the Mark II, an early computer, and caused a short circuit. Grace Hopper and her co-workers pulled it out with tweezers. They taped their "computer bug" into the log book. Afterward they told their boss they were "debugging" the computer.[1]

Grace Hopper did much more than invent colorful phrases. She programmed some of the first computers. She contributed to the development of Common Business-Oriented Language (COBOL), a computer language. Early on, she realized that computers were essential. Through teaching and in speeches, she told people how important computers could be. She served in the Navy and the Naval Reserve for more than forty years. There, she reached the rank of rear admiral. For several years, she had the rare honor of being the oldest Naval officer on active duty.

This remarkable woman was born in New York City on December 9, 1906. Grace Brewster Murray was the oldest child of Walter Fletcher Murray and Mary Campbell Van Horne Murray. She had one brother, Roger, and one sister, Mary.

Grace's grandfather was a civil engineer for New York. From him, she learned to love maps. When he measured for new streets, she tagged along and held the surveyor's pole.

Grace had a happy childhood growing up in New York City.[2] She went to private schools, where she was good at mathematics. She especially liked geometry.[3] The family spent summers in New Hampshire.

Grace was fascinated with how machines run. One day her mother found all the alarm clocks in their summer home in pieces:

> What had happened was that I'd taken the first one apart and I couldn't get it together so I opened the next one. I ended up with all seven of them apart. After that I was restricted to one clock. It's that kind of curiosity: How do things work?[4]

When Grace was a teenager, many people did not approve of education for women. Yet Hopper's father was different. He wanted his daughters to go to college. So Grace went off to Vassar, an all-female college. After graduating in 1928, she earned her master's degree in 1930 from Yale University. That same year she married Vincent Foster Hopper. (They divorced in 1945.) She returned to Vassar as a math professor, teaching there from 1931 to 1944. She also went on to earn a Ph.D. in mathematics from Yale in 1934.

During World War II (1939–1945), many young women were eager to join the Navy, including Grace Hopper. Females were not allowed to serve aboard any ship. Yet women could enlist in the Women Accepted for Volunteer Emergency Service (WAVES). After training, Grace became Lieutenant Hopper.

She was assigned to the Bureau of Ordnance Computation Project. Part of her job was to calculate firing distances for weapons. She worked at Harvard University. Here, the Navy ran a computer, the Mark I. Grace had never seen a computer before. She recalled, "I've always loved a good gadget. When I met Mark I, it was the biggest, fanciest gadget I'd ever seen. I had to find out how it worked."[5]

Mark I was huge: fifty-one feet long. Its computing power, though, was slow. It could do three additions each second. (By 2011, a supercomputer could do 8.2 quadrillion calculations per second—about the same as one million desktop computers linked together.)[6] Still for the time, it was amazing. Hopper quickly learned how Mark I worked. She wrote some of its early programs and the user's manual.

Computers were not yet used in many places. Yet Hopper believed that they would be good at work other than the military. The business uses of computers began to attract her. Her technical skills were in demand, so she wrote some programs for companies. She developed a knack for marketing too. Soon, she knew, companies would have to rely on fast, accurate, computing machines.

In 1946, Hopper retired from the Navy. She stayed at Harvard to work on the Mark II and Mark III. With this background, she went into the business world. She took a job as a mathematician at Eckert-Mauchly Computer Corporation in Philadelphia. There, J. Presper Eckert, Jr., and John W. Mauchly were building Universal Automatic Computer (UNIVAC I).

In business, as in the Navy, Hopper was a determined problem-solver. She might be told something could not be done. If she thought it could, she went right ahead and tried. She liked to say, "It's much easier to apologize than it is to get permission."[7]

With her staff, Hopper wrote the first compiler. In this type of computer program, the programmer's code is changed into the computer's code.

The programmer's code is in words. The machine's code is binary—made up of 1s and 0s. A compiler, then, is like a translator. It changes instructions that a human programmer could understand into code that the machine could understand.

Hopper's compilers influenced the development of COBOL. This language made it easy for business programmers, who were usually not mathematicians, to program their computers.

Feisty Hopper always let her opinions be known. She was especially outspoken about the need for standards in computer languages, just as there are standard weights or tool sizes.

Through the years, Hopper still served proudly in the United States Naval Reserve. She moved up in rank from lieutenant to lieutenant commander, then to commander. At that rank, she retired in 1966. She called it "the saddest day of my life."[8]

By the next year, she was back on active duty. The Navy needed her help with its software. She did not retire from teaching either. Colleges invited her to give lectures and to be a visiting professor. In fact, of all her achievements, she was most proud of the people she helped educate.[9]

Grace Hopper became a captain in the Navy in 1973. Based in Washington, D.C., she traveled all over the world. She spoke at many schools and conventions. Sometimes she talked about things that were hard to understand. Then she used examples. To explain nanosecond (one billionth of a second),

Grace Hopper moved easily between the government and business worlds, between programming and teaching. Many people called her *Amazing Grace*.

she gave each listener a piece of telephone cable. The length of the cable showed how far electricity could travel in one nanosecond (11.75 inches!).[10]

Hopper received many awards, both in the United States and abroad. In 1982, she earned a unique honor: She became the oldest Naval officer on active duty.

Although work kept her busy, Hopper took up a hobby: genealogy. Her mother had started research into the family tree. After her mother died, Hopper took over and traced her family back to colonial times.

Personal computers were now starting to show up in homes and businesses across the country. Hopper compared the PCs in the computer industry to the Model T's in the auto industry:

> After we began to get the Model T's, we blacktopped the roads, we built concrete roads, people moved to the suburbs. It was the beginning of a whole new world. I think you can say that the microcomputers are the Model T's—people can own them. . . . Goodness only knows what'll happen afterwards, because when we got the Model T, you couldn't have dreamed of a 747.[11]

In 1986, Hopper, now a rear admiral, took her final retirement from the Navy. A special ceremony was held on a summer day in Boston Harbor. The oldest officer retired on board the oldest commissioned ship. The U.S.S. *Constitution,* nicknamed "Old Ironsides," dates back to 1797. Hopper was seventy-nine years old.

Still, she did not quit working. Digital Equipment Corporation hired her. She kept right on traveling and speaking, now for a computer company.

Even in her eighties, she was a champion for change. One of her favorite sayings was, "A ship in port is safe, but that is not what ships are built for."[12] In her office, Hopper kept a clock that ran counterclockwise. She used it to show that there is always more than one way to do anything. She made sure the people who worked for her did the same: "They come to me, you know, and say, 'Do you think we can do this?' I say, 'Try it.' And I back 'em up. They need that. . . . I stir 'em up at intervals so they don't forget to take chances."[13]

Grace Murray Hopper died on January 1, 1992, at her home in Arlington, Virginia. In the history of computing, she is the most famous American woman. She worked with computers for more than forty years. In that time, she saw them change from big, slow machines to sleek, laptop-sized wonders. As a programmer, she knew the hardware and software. As a teacher, she made computers easier to understand. Her work made these tools user-friendly parts of everyday life.

4

John W. Mauchly and J. Presper Eckert, Jr.

Builders of ENIAC and UNIVAC

Can people be computers? During World War II, they were. Young women at the Ballistic Research Laboratory were called "computers." They worked out firing tables for the Army (how far a bullet or missile would go under different conditions). Their tools were a mechanical calculator, paper, and pencil. With the war raging, the need for these weapons statistics grew daily. Soon, not even two hundred human computers could keep up with the demand.

At the University of Pennsylvania, two men had an idea. John W. Mauchly [mawk-lee] and J. Presper Eckert, Jr., designed a machine that could do in seconds what took humans hours. The machine was the Electronic Numerical Integrator and Computer (ENIAC). This was just the first

James R. Wiener; J. Presper Eckert, Jr.; and Dr. John W. Mauchly, look over the memory section of the Mauchly-Eckert Corp. computer on August 30, 1949.

machine they would produce together. They went on to invent three more major computers and to set up the very first computer company.

Both Mauchly and Eckert's backgrounds prepared them for their future partnership. Even their childhoods pointed them toward a lifetime of invention.

John William Mauchly was born on August 30, 1907, in Cincinnati, Ohio. His father was a physicist. John experimented with electricity even as a young boy. When he was just five, he built a flashlight. Later, he invented a device that turned off his reading lamp when his mother came up the stairs (and turned it back on when she went down). For an April Fool's joke, he rigged his doorbell so visitors would get a mild shock.[1]

Mauchly began college studying electrical engineering, but he later switched to physics. In 1930, he married Mary Walzl. Two years later, he earned a Ph.D. from Johns Hopkins University. He then became a professor at Ursinus College, near Philadelphia. To his students, Mauchly was a good teacher with a lively sense of humor.[2]

Mauchly was very interested in meteorology. To study the weather, he had to do many calculations. He began to think of a device that would help him figure this math quickly.

When World War II started, Mauchly quit teaching. He became a student again at the Moore School of Electrical Engineering. This school at the

University of Pennsylvania had hired young Pres Eckert to teach an electronics course.

John Presper Eckert, Jr., came from a family background that was different from his future partner's. He was born on April 9, 1919, in Philadelphia. His family was in real estate and tried to push him toward a career in business. Yet even as a child, he was an inventor and scientist. He built a crystal radio set on a pencil at age eight.[3] When he was twelve, he won first prize in a hobby fair with his magnetized boat. In high school, he made a bomb explode on stage with a push-button remote control while sitting in the audience.[4]

Eckert was an only child whose parents were quite wealthy. Their circle of friends included the president of the United States and movie stars, such as Charlie Chaplin. Their son did so well in his studies that he took college math in high school. Accepted by Massachusetts Institute of Technology (MIT), Eckert instead went reluctantly to the Moore School, because his mother wanted him nearby.[5]

Throughout his college years, he designed instruments and devices. Some were used in the war. He was a lab instructor and still a student when he taught the electronics course that John Mauchly took.

The class was pretty basic for Mauchly. He finished the lab exercises quickly; then he and Eckert had plenty of time to discuss their interests.

Mauchly told Eckert about his idea for an electronic computer. Together, they convinced the Moore School to let them build it there.

The work began in 1943. ENIAC was built under an Army contract. The purpose of the machine was to figure those endless calculations that the human "computers" were doing. The Army needed even more weapons data, because the war had spread to North Africa.

Because it was a military project, the plan was secret. Its code name was Project PX. "One could not discuss one's own work with others, whether friends or staff, . . . unless they too were 'cleared' for the same project. They were probably cleared for something, but if for a different project, that was not enough," Mauchly remembered.[6]

This secrecy meant the pair could not publish anything about their work, which scientists do to spread ideas. It also caused problems for Eckert. At twenty-four years old, he was the right age to be drafted into the Army. The local draft board decided who could be exempted. Board members had no idea of the importance of his work for the war effort. Finally, the school and government made sure Eckert was kept home working on ENIAC.

The planning and building of ENIAC took about two and a half years. Besides program errors and loose knobs, mice were a problem. They thought the wires were tasty. So the scientists caught a few of the rodents. After several days without food, the mice were given different kinds of wire to eat. If they gobbled up one kind, it would not be used. But, if they refused to eat another kind, it was installed.[7]

What did the first electronic computer look like? It was a massive machine. Weighing thirty tons, it contained eighteen-thousand vacuum tubes and six-thousand switches. Operators ran around the forty panels to check switches and connect wires. What they were doing was programming the computer. It did not have a stored program.

Four thousand red neon lights blinked on the machine. These alerted operators to a problem. They stayed on in the public's imagination too. Eckert recalled, ". . . every computer I've seen in a science fiction movie since this machine came out had flashing lights."[8]

By early 1946, ENIAC was ready. In a demonstration of its power, it performed five-thousand additions in a second and five-hundred multiplications in a second. It also computed a problem for the top-secret hydrogen bomb project. Because World War II was now over, the military had new plans for ENIAC. Of course, Eckert and Mauchly had always thought that their computer would have more than one use.[9]

Now they wanted to build a new machine. It would feature a stored-program memory. During the project, they worked with John von Neumann. However, their computer, Electronic Discrete Variable Automatic Computer (EDVAC), was not built by the team. Mauchly and Eckert left the Moore School in 1946, because the university wanted their patent rights for ENIAC and EDVAC. So the two started their own business, the Electronic Control Company. (Later it became the Eckert-Mauchly Computer Corporation.) This was the first computer company. Unfortunately, the two were better scientists than businessmen. The company often ran short of money.

In 1946, Mauchly also faced personal loss. His wife, Mary, drowned during a swim at a New Jersey beach. In time, Mauchly married Kathleen McNulty, one of the human "computers" during the war.

Eckert and Mauchly's new company began with a government contract. For the Air Force, the team built the Binary Automatic Computer (BINAC). Yet BINAC was just a stepping-stone to the computer that was to change the industry—the Universal Automatic Computer (UNIVAC).[10]

The United States Census Bureau bought the first UNIVAC. The bureau had been using some form of Herman Hollerith's tabulating machine for more than half a century. It was time to go modern for the 1950 count. UNIVAC used magnetic tapes rather than punch cards.

Then, in 1952, UNIVAC made history. It was a presidential election year. Newspaper polls predicted that Adlai Stevenson would defeat Dwight D. Eisenhower. For the first time, a computer forecast the outcome from the early returns. It was broadcast on TV. With just a small sample, UNIVAC predicted that

This 1946 photograph shows ENIAC, a thirty-ton electronic machine at the University of Pennsylvania. In the 1980s, the National Society of Professional Engineers named ENIAC as one of the ten most outstanding engineering achievements of the past fifty years.

Eisenhower would win over Stevenson by a wide margin. At first, the TV network and computer people thought that the computer made a mistake. However, UNIVAC was right, and Eisenhower was elected.

Despite this success, money problems strained the Eckert-Mauchly company. They sold their firm to Remington Rand, which later became Sperry Rand and then Unisys.

Mauchly worked for Remington Rand, then set up his own company, Mauchly Associates, in 1959. He died January 8, 1980, during heart surgery. He left behind his wife, Kathleen, and seven children.

Eckert married Judith Rewalt and had four children. He worked for Rand until he retired. He died on June 3, 1995, of leukemia.

As a team, Mauchly and Eckert were perfectly matched. The brilliant Eckert was a no-nonsense engineer who could come across as gruff. Mauchly was outgoing and friendly. Mauchly could imagine what might be; Eckert could engineer it.[11]

The machines they envisioned and built paved the way for commercial use of computers. Computer scientists can point to ENIAC as the first working electronic computer that was fast and accurate.

Years after, Eckert said, "What puzzles me is that there wasn't anything in the ENIAC . . . that wasn't available 10 or 15 years earlier. The real question is, 'Why wasn't it done sooner?'"[12]

Perhaps it just took this special team to bring it all together.

5

An Wang

"Find a Need and Fill It"

With just $600 in savings, An Wang started a small business. He was a young man with a wife, a baby son, a patent, and lots of confidence. Over the years, he built Wang Laboratories into a major computer company. In 1951, the company had just one employee—An Wang. But, by the 1980s, it had thousands of workers and was worth several billion dollars.

On February 7, 1920, An Wang was born in Shanghai, China. His parents were Yin Lu and Zen Wan (Chien) Wang. He had an older sister, Hsu; a younger sister, Yu; and younger brothers, Ping and Ge. His father taught English at a school in the nearby village of Kun San, where the family moved when Wang was six.

Dr. An Wang

In the 1920s, China bristled with tension. After thousands of years of rule by emperors, revolution was in the air. Warlords gained control, and many people feared for their lives. Yet the Wangs were safe in the little town, and An was ready to start school. Because there was no first or second grade, he began in third and so was always two years younger than his classmates. Of all his subjects, he found math easiest. He also studied English at school and with his father.

In the small library at Kun San, he read many books. "[B]y reading I learned a lot about the world beyond my town and even beyond China,"[1] he recalled. When it was time for high school, Wang's parents sent him to one of the best in China, Shanghai Provincial High School. There, some of his textbooks were in English, so he learned even more of what would become his second language.

With the highest entrance-exam score in his class, he entered Chiao Tung University. There, he studied electrical engineering. The school had a table-tennis team, which he joined. He also translated articles in American science magazines into Chinese.

By this time, war between China and Japan seemed certain. Wang was fairly safe at school, because the university had been moved to a French-owned area. In 1937, Japan invaded China. World War II had started for the Chinese. Wang's father and older sister died during the war; Wang never found out how. His mother also died, her health shattered by the stress of the war.

At the age of twenty, Wang graduated. He remembered later, "I . . . felt that it was time I made my contribution to the war effort."[2] Using his engineering skills, he designed radios that were used by Chinese troops. By 1941, no place in Japanese-occupied Shanghai was safe, so Wang and a few others slipped through enemy lines at night. By boat, train, and foot, they trekked until they were far into China. They still suffered through bombing raids, but it was safer than Shanghai.

When the war ended in 1945, Wang applied to a program that brought Chinese engineers to the United States for training. He came to Harvard University. With a good academic background and his practical experience during the war, he did well in classes. By 1946, he earned his master's in applied physics. A Ph.D. followed sixteen months later.

Wang liked living in the United States and knew he would stay. He went to work at Harvard's Computation Laboratory. This was the home of the Mark I, one of the first computers. When he was assigned to research a way to store information, he worked at the problem. From this effort came a great result: He invented a magnetic memory core. A series of doughnut-shaped magnets hung on copper wire. Each magnet (core) stored a bit of data. It became the standard for the computer industry until the microchip was invented.

Still, life was not all work. Wang mingled with other Chinese researchers and students at parties.

At one party, he met Lorraine Chiu. She was studying English literature at Wellesley College and was also from Shanghai. In 1949, they married.

The same year, Wang filed for a patent for his invention. That plus articles he had written soon made him well known in the electronics field. He considered leaving Harvard's Lab and starting his own business. With his reputation as an electronics expert, he thought he could become a success.[3]

Wang Laboratories began in June 1951. In an empty building in South Boston, Wang set up shop. He called research people he knew, mailed information to companies, and went to trade shows. He began selling the memory cores, and his business grew. He branched out into doing design projects for customers. He kept up his own research, tinkering with improvements on his designs. Wang marketed new uses for the memory cores. One of the first digital scoreboards—at Shea Stadium in New York—was programmed with the cores.

Wang's family was growing too. Two boys, Fred and Courtney, and a girl, Juliette, were born. The children were American citizens, because they were born in the United States. An and Lorraine Wang became citizens in 1955.

Wang Laboratories kept up a steady growth. Wang learned to be a businessman as well as an engineer. He believed that good business judgment was just as important as technical knowledge.[4]

Then, in 1965, Wang brought out the logarithmic calculating instrument (LOCI). LOCI was a desktop calculator. In the days before pocket calculators and personal computers, LOCI brought the power of big mainframes to a desk. It could add, subtract, multiply, and divide. It figured roots and logarithms. Scientists and engineers liked these features and the fact that it could be programmed. With only a few keystrokes, they had an answer.[5]

Next came the Model 300. It was designed for business users rather than for scientists. With it, Wang's business boomed. In 1964, thirty-five people worked for Wang; in 1967, more than four hundred were employed. The company moved to new quarters, which soon had to be expanded.

Even with this huge success, Wang knew that calculators would not always be profit makers.[6] So he began plans to design and market a computer. At about this time, magnetic-core memory was on its way out. Something new had struck the electronics field—the chip. A semiconductor chip stored more memory than a magnetic core. Wang became the first customer of Intel, the company that sold these chips. (Intel is would go on to produce Pentium™ processors.)

By 1970, Wang Laboratories employed fourteen hundred people, and sales were $27 million. The company began to change from being famous for calculators to being known for computers. Soon Wang brought out a word processor.

Dr. An Wang, Chinese-born American executive and electronics engineer, who founded Wang Laboratories, a major contributor in the field of computer technology is shown here.

Word processing made typing easier. A user simply hit commands on the keyboard to add or delete. Wang felt, " . . . secretarial work was real drudgery. If you made typing mistakes, you would have to retype the entire document. So why not put the information on a screen where it could be easily erased and edited?"[7]

With these computers, Wang competed against IBM, the computer giant. Clever TV ads played up the little-company-taking-on-the-huge-one theme. To prove how serious he was, Wang put his son Fred in charge of sales of the word processors in 1976. Word processing took the company to $1 billion in sales in 1982.

As computers became a fixture in offices, Wang expanded its line. Companies wanted computers that could do more than one thing. Could one computer handle data and word processing? Could several terminals form a network so they could "talk" to a central computer? Wang sold personal computers (PCs), which were becoming popular with companies.

By 1986, Wang Laboratories was a $3-billion company with thirty thousand employees. Wang was a wealthy—and very generous—man. His workers called him "the Doctor." He believed in giving back to the community that had helped him.[8] With his wife, Wang discussed where they could do the most good.

He gave money to Harvard. He founded the Wang Institute of Graduate Studies, which offered classes in high-tech subjects and East Asian studies. His money built the outpatient unit of Massachusetts General Hospital. When the performing-arts center in Boston needed repairs, the Wangs donated $4 million. That, with matching donations from others, saved the place, and it was renamed the Wang Theatre.

Although the company slumped in the 1980s, Wang continued to lead. He appointed a president, John Cunningham, to handle marketing. Wang himself controlled manufacturing and research and development.[9] Later he took back the title of president and, in 1986, made his son Fred president. Wang had to make many hard decisions as business went flat. He removed Fred and made Richard Miller president in 1989.

An Wang died on March 24, 1990, of cancer. The company went through some tough times, including bankruptcy. In 1993, it made a comeback, concentrating on software and service.[10] In 1997, the company was bought by Eastman Kodak.

Wang's company always followed the motto "Find a need and fill it."[11] An Wang produced scientific instruments, business machines, data processors, and word processors to fill companies' needs. As a scientist and businessman, he embraced it all. As he remembered, "My education, my research . . . and my career . . . have all been enormous fun. My days are spent doing the things I really want to do. The satisfaction of turning an idea into something real never diminishes."[12]

6

Jack Kilby and Robert Noyce

Inventors of the Chip That Changed the World

With the remote control, you switch on the TV to a show on cable. You check your digital smartphone for messages. Then, you pick up a slice of pizza that you prepared in the microwave.

Jack Kilby and Robert Noyce helped you with your food and fun. Their invention, the microchip, unleashed the power of computers. In the sky, satellites bounce television and smartphone signals to Earth. In the kitchen, ovens "nuke" food with microwaves. Homes, offices, factories, and hospitals are filled with products Kilby and Noyce made possible. The chip is everywhere.

Jack St. Clair Kilby was born on November 8, 1923, in Jefferson City, Missouri. His parents, Hubert and Vina, moved to Kansas when Jack was

Jack Kilby poses with his original 1958 invention, the world's first integrated circuit, encased in a glass cover, at the United States pavilion at the 1985 Science Exposition in Tsukuba, Japan.

four years old. His father was an engineer for power companies in the Midwest. They settled in Great Bend, Kansas. Jack went to school there, where American history was his favorite subject.[1]

During a blizzard in 1937, Kilby saw his father use an amateur radio when phone lines were downed. He tried it himself. Intrigued, he earned his ham-radio license and built his own set.

Kilby wanted to be an electrical engineer. After high school, he tested for Massachusetts Institute of Technology (MIT), the famous engineering school. He missed the passing score by three points. So he headed for the University of Illinois in 1941. Late that year, the United States entered World War II. Corporal Kilby was sent to India to work with radio transmitters.

College was waiting for Kilby when he returned from the war. He earned his electrical engineering degree in electrical engineering in 1947. Hired by Centralab in Milwaukee, Wisconsin, he worked on transistors. He also earned a master's degree in electrical engineering from the University of Wisconsin.

After eleven years, Kilby decided to take a job with the electronics company Texas Instruments (TI). TI was the first to make silicon transistors. Kilby; his wife, Barbara; and their two daughters, Ann and Janet Lee, packed up for Dallas.

Soon after Kilby arrived, TI shut down for the annual summer vacation. Because he was new and had not yet earned vacation time, Kilby had to go in and work. A friendly, easygoing man, he still liked to work things through on his own.[2] On July 24, 1958, he opened his lab notebook. Kilby wrote: "The following circuit elements could be made on a single slice: resistors, capacitor, distributed capacitor, transistor."[3] The circuit would be one single unit. (At the time they were on circuit boards, which were big and bulky.) Kilby's idea, hatched in the deserted lab, was about to change the field of electronics.

When his boss came back from vacation, Kilby showed him his notes for building an integrated circuit (IC). He was told he could work on it if he could show that it might succeed. He wired a silicon resistor and a silicon capacitor into a circuit. When that worked, he produced an IC on one chip. In September, he demonstrated it to company executives. It worked!

Yet the chip was not at all ready to be produced and sold. As Kilby recalled, "[I]t was pretty crude."[4] Interconnecting the components was a problem. Kilby had used small gold wires, which he applied by hand. This method would not be practical for mass production. Despite that, on February 6, 1959, the application for a patent was sent to the United States Patent Office.

Meanwhile, in California, another engineer was working on the same idea. Robert Noyce is considered coinventor of the microchip with Jack Kilby. Kilby's dated notebooks show that he first developed an IC. Noyce solved the interconnection problem.

Born in the city of Burlington, Iowa, on December 12, 1927, Robert Norton Noyce was the son of a minister. The Noyce family, with four boys, moved a lot. Young Robert loved to tinker and experiment. He built model planes with radio control units. He attached a washing machine engine to his bike.

In high school, Noyce showed talent in math and physics. His family had settled in Grinnell, Iowa, and he went to Grinnell College. In physics class, he saw one of the first transistors. Noyce was immediately impressed. Besides his scientific interests, he tried many other activities. He joined the swim team and became a star diver. He sang and played oboe. He was even an actor on a radio soap opera.

For one activity, though, Noyce landed in a heap of trouble. Late at night, he and a friend stole a pig from a farm for a Hawaiian luau. To the farmer, this was no prank; it was a crime. Noyce's father and a professor kept him from jail, but he was suspended for one semester.

He returned to school and graduated with his class in 1949. Then, he moved east to earn a Ph.D. from MIT in 1953. From several job offers, he chose Philco and began working in its transistor division. While there, he wrote some scientific papers on semiconductors.

One day in 1956, William Shockley, one of the inventors of the transistor, called Noyce. He asked the young electronics whiz if he wanted to work in a company he was starting. Noyce; his wife, Betty; and their children moved from Philadelphia to Mountain View, California.

After just a few months, Noyce and his fellow workers were unhappy. Shockley, though a Nobel Prize winner, was not an easy man to work for; he did not seem to trust anyone. So a group of eight left in 1957 to start their own business, Fairchild Semiconductor Corporation. Noyce's leadership skills made him the natural choice to head the company.

The company was run in a new way that influenced many future start-up companies. No special offices or parking spaces were given to executives. Anyone with an idea could talk to Noyce and not have to go through bosses in between. Noyce was an outgoing, talkative man who liked to sift through ideas aloud.[5]

Fairchild made silicon transistors. Noyce thought about the same problem Kilby had: how to integrate circuits. On January 23, 1959, he wrote in his notebook, ". . . it would be desirable to make multiple devices on a single piece of silicon. . . ."[6]

Noyce designed a chip without wires. Connections were made with lines of metal printed on silicon plates (later called printed circuit boards). He filed the patent for this IC on July 30, 1959. Patent applications go through the process at different speeds, and Noyce's patent was awarded before Kilby's.

At Texas Instruments, lawyers filed papers to claim that Kilby was the IC's first inventor. "*Kilby versus Noyce*" had begun and would continue for ten years. In the end, Fairchild and Texas Instruments made a deal. They agreed that each had made prime contributions to the IC. They would grant licenses to each other and jointly to any other company that wanted to produce chips. The inventors themselves and other scientists agreed that Kilby and Noyce deserved joint credit.[7]

ICs were ready for the world outside the lab. First used by the government, they flew in *Apollo* spacecraft and the Minuteman missile. Today the chips can be found in thousands of everyday devices, from advanced computers to electronic toys.

Yet at the time, as Kilby recalls, "We thought it might be important to electronics then. What we didn't foresee was the tremendous decrease in cost . . . a one million to one drop. That allowed electronics in many more products."[8]

Kilby went on to invent the pocket calculator. He left TI in 1970 and became a self-employed inventor and consultant.[9] He officially retired in 1983. His inventions have yielded more than sixty patents. He died on June 20, 2005, in Dallas, after battling cancer.

Noyce left Fairchild in 1968. With another Fairchild founder, Gordon Moore, he began Intel Corporation. They hired many Ph.D.s to do research on chip applications. At one point, Noyce

Robert Noyce became known as the "Mayor of Silicon Valley" for his untiring work to improve the semiconductor industry and its markets.

told his workers not to page these researchers by their title "Doctor," because "[t]he office was beginning to sound too much like a hospital."[10]

Computers at the time used core memories. Noyce and Moore were convinced that semiconductors, smaller and cheaper, could replace the core devices.[11] The company took off; however, his marriage ended. He and Betty divorced in 1974. The next year he married Ann Bowers, an Intel employee.

Noyce led the company until 1979, when he became vice chairman. He used his spare time to speak out for the semiconductor industry. His enthusiasm and energy led some to call him the Mayor of Silicon Valley.

He moved to Austin, Texas, to head Sematech. This group of semiconductor manufacturers tries to strengthen the American market and improve microchip companies. He died on June 3, 1990, after a heart attack.

They were both inducted into the National Inventors' Hall of Fame. In 2000, Kilby was awarded the Nobel Prize in physics "for his part in inventing the integrated circuit."[12] Like Thomas Edison, the Wright brothers, and Alexander Graham Bell, Kilby and Noyce invented an irreplaceable tool of modern life. Chips are in personal computers, cars, video games, store scanners, cellular phones, TVs, clocks, and much more. Because of Kilby and Noyce, electronics—and the world—changed forever.

7

Bill Gates

"A Computer on Every Desk and in Every Home"

The news spread quickly among the students at Lakeside. There was a computer in the school! For Bill Gates, an eighth grader in 1968, this was great news. Computers, rare in schools at the time, gave him a new challenge. Learning about programming was fun for him. Soon he was spending all his free time at the computer.

Even as a teenager, Gates knew enough about computers to start a company. By the time he was nineteen, he and a partner had formed Microsoft, which would become the biggest software company ever.

William Henry Gates III was born on October 28, 1955, in the city of Seattle, Washington. His parents were respected and active in their community. His

Bill Gates

father, William Henry Gates, Jr., was a lawyer. Mary Maxwell Gates, his mother, was a teacher before her children were born. Young Bill had an older sister, Kristianne, and a younger sister, Libby.

Bill, nicknamed "Trey" for "the third" in his name, was a very bright boy. Grade school often bored him. He earned good grades in math and reading, which he liked. Yet in classes in which he was not interested, he made Cs and Ds.[1] And he was full of energy.

William Jr., and Mary searched for activities for their son. He joined Boy Scouts, learned tennis and skiing, had a paper route, and spent active summers with friends. His parents, worried about increasing behavior problems at school,[2] entered him in Lakeside, an all-boys' private school. There, small gawky Bill, "a nerd before the term was invented,"[3] as a teacher remembered him, came into his own. The computer helped. Donated by the Lakeside Mothers' Club, the time-share machine hooked into an off-site mainframe with hundreds of users.

Gates and fellow student Paul Allen soon passed their teachers in computer knowledge. They cut classes to use the machine. They wanted to learn everything they could about it. This was not at all like a modern personal computer (PC). No screen displayed what was typed. Students worked at a keyboard and a teletype printer. Gates remembers: "I wrote my first software program when I was thirteen years old. It was for playing tic-tac-toe.

The computer I was using was huge and cumbersome and slow and absolutely compelling."[4]

Because they used so much computer time, Gates and Allen had to pay for some of it themselves. They looked for programming jobs. The best were jobs that paid in cash and in computer time.

Working for Computer Center Corporation, Gates looked for "bugs" in the system. He also learned to "crash" programs, which brought them to a sudden stop. At one point, he went too far: He crashed a Control Data Corporation system just to prove that he could do it. He was caught and banned from computers for a time.

Gates even worked for Lakeside. He wrote a program to handle the complex job of scheduling classes. Lakeside had by then gone coed. Gates managed to schedule himself into classes as the only boy with all girls.

One day Allen showed Gates an ad for an Intel chip. The boys bought the 8008 chip for $360. Gates had a plan: "We thought we could use the 8008 as the heart of a special computer to do traffic-volume-count analysis. We were going to make the machines and sell them to traffic departments. So we set up our first company, which we called Traf-O-Data."[5]

They did sell some units. Then sales dropped when buyers found out the company was run by teens. But Traf-O-Data taught the partners much about microprocessors and business.

Gates was still in high school, where he acted in plays and impressed teachers with his memory. He was constantly moving; even when sitting, he rocked back and forth. His excess energy helped when he stayed up all night "hacking code."

In the summer of 1972, Gates served as a page for the United States House of Representatives. Many future lawyers and politicians work as pages. Gates's parents wanted him to go to college. He decided on Harvard University near Boston. There, he was humbled to find people who were smarter than he was in math.[6]

Allen had dropped out of college to take a programming job. He eventually came to Boston too. (Boston was the center of the minicomputer industry.) The two friends discussed what kind of business they could start.

Then, in late 1974, Allen picked up a copy of the January 1975 *Popular Electronics*. On the cover was the Altair, the "world's first minicomputer kit." Inside he found out that it was now possible to build a computer for less than $400. ". . . Allen ran through Harvard Square with the article to wave it in front of Gates's face and say, 'Look, it's going to happen! I told you this was going to happen! And we're going to miss it!'"[7]

Gates remembers reading about that first personal computer: ". . . Paul and I didn't know exactly how it would be used, but we were sure it would change us and the world of computing. We were right."[8]

They decided to start a software company. They began to write a program for the Altair. Gates went on leave from Harvard. With lots of work and little sleep, they exhausted themselves.

Without even seeing an Altair, the two wrote BASIC (a computer language) for it. They called Ed Roberts, founder of MITS, the company that built the Altair. Gates told him what they had done. Allen took the program to Albuquerque, New Mexico, home of MITS.

Would it work? The program, on punched paper tape, was fed into the computer. As Allen and Roberts watched, the word READY came out of the printing device. Gates's eight thousand lines of code had done it! Roberts, ready to sell BASIC with his machine, hired Allen. Gates also moved to Albuquerque. They worked to improve their product.

Microsoft Corporation was in business. Their contract with MITS let Gates and Allen own their software as it was leased to users. Gates realized that they were at the beginning of a revolution: "By the time we got to Albuquerque to start Microsoft in 1975, the notion was fairly clear to us that computers were going to be a big, big personal tool."[9]

In the early days of the company, they wrote software for other computers, too, and sold hardware. The home computer industry grew explosively, and Microsoft with it. In 1979, the company moved to Bellevue, Washington.

A deal with IBM in 1980 made both companies big players in the personal computer market. Microsoft wrote Microsoft® Disk Operating System (MS-DOS) for IBM. Other companies bought licenses for it, benefiting IBM and Microsoft.

Gates was brilliant and ambitious.[10] He also had an instant-recall memory and the ability to understand the law,[11] which helped in business. His programmers worked the way he did: long hours, seven days a week, forgetting to eat, sometimes sleeping on the office floor. They were a close-knit group.

Then in 1982, the closeness was threatened. Doctors told Allen he had Hodgkin's disease, a form of cancer. After undergoing therapy, he decided he could not go back to the more-than-full-time work at Microsoft. He remained a friend and advisor to Gates while pursuing new goals for himself. Among other accomplishments, he funded SpaceShipOne, the first nongovernment effort to send people into space. With his sister Jo Lynn Allen, he also started the Allen Institute for Brain Science and the Paul G. Allen Family Foundation.

Microsoft grew at an incredible rate. In 1986, it moved to Redmond, Washington. By the time he was thirty-one, Gates was a billionaire. Yet he did not act as if he had a lot of money. He wore the same style of clothes—a pull-over sweater with a shirt and slacks. He did not take long vacations. He ran his big company as if it were small, with teams working on each project.

Microsoft's mission was "A computer on every desk and in every home."[12] With multimedia CD-ROMs and such programs as Microsoft® Windows, he commanded the leading software company in the world. Gates was achieving his goal.

Gates also began Corbis. This company collects photographs, then converts them into digital images. Gates knows that "quality images will be in great demand on the [information] highway."[13]

When Netscape burst onto the Internet scene with its Netscape® Navigator, Gates took notice. Microsoft brought out Microsoft® Internet Explorer, its Web browser, in 1996.

Gates also ventured into the cable TV business. With NBC he created MSNBC, a news service on cable and the Internet.

Meanwhile, people wondered whether he would stop working long enough to have a personal life. On January 1, 1994, he married Melinda French, who also worked at Microsoft. Their daughter , Jennifer, was born in 1996, son Rory in 1999, and daughter Phoebe in 2002. Together, the couple started the Bill & Melinda Gates Foundation, which has given billions of dollars to charity. In 2010, they pledged to donate 95 percent of their wealth to charity.[14]

Although Bill Gates stepped down as Microsoft's CEO in January 2000, he stayed on as Chief Software Architect until he retired on June 27, 2008. His company has continued to grow, adding and

A young Bill Gates relaxes at Lakeside School. There he first used a computer, which started him on his career as head of Microsoft.

updating core products, such as Microsoft® Office, which is software for home and business use; the Windows® operating system; the Windows® Phone operating system; and its XBox® gaming platform.

Because he could imagine the future, Gates blazed the trail for the personal computer. He continues to look forward:

> I'm actually quite envious of kids growing up today. They won't have to go through all the things we've gone through. In fact, when we look back at today's personal computer, I think we'll say these were the machines that couldn't listen, couldn't talk, . . . the tools kids will have to pursue their curiosity will be quite amazing.[15]

And Microsoft, the technical giant begun by master businessman Bill Gates, will be sure to provide those tools.

8

Steve Jobs and Steve Wozniak

Computers for the People

Late one night, the phone rang at the Vatican. An American diplomat wanted to talk to the pope. As someone rushed to wake the pope, a translator talked to the American. He soon realized this was no diplomat. The call was a prank.

At the other end of the line, Steve Wozniak could not help laughing. He had hacked the phone company's computers. And he had pulled off a joke that he would talk about for years.

Pranks and a love of electronics brought Steve Jobs and Steve Wozniak (also known as Woz) together. Yet behind the practical jokes, the two made a powerhouse team. They built and sold one of the first personal computers, the Apple. Its user-friendly features made Apple a favorite with many people.

Steve Wozniak (left) and Steve Jobs

The two Steves were raised in what is now called Silicon Valley. Steven Paul Jobs was born on February 24, 1955, in San Francisco. He was adopted by Paul and Clara Jobs. Two years later, they adopted again. Now Steve had a little sister, Patty.

In 1961, the Jobs family moved to Mountain View. Paul Jobs worked for a finance company. He also loved to tinker with cars. His son never seemed interested in working on engines but often went along to sell a car or buy used parts. From his dad, Steve learned to make deals and know prices.[1]

Young Steve was bright, but a challenge for his parents and teachers. He liked to question authority. His favorite hobbies were electronics and swimming. Northern California was a great place for a kid who liked electronics. Many engineers worked in companies there and worked at home too. Hanging around the garages and workshops of these neighbors, Steve learned about batteries, circuits, and silicon.

One of the companies, Hewlett-Packard, sponsored a club for kids. At a meeting, Steve Jobs first saw a computer. He remembered, "I was maybe 12 the first time. . . . They showed us one of their new desktop computers and let us play on it. I wanted one badly. I thought they were neat."[2]

Meanwhile, at swimming practices and meets, Clara Jobs met Margaret Wozniak. Margaret; her husband, Jerry; and their three children, Steve, Leslie, and Mark, lived in the city of Sunnyvale.

Their oldest son, Stephen Gary, was born on August 11, 1950, in San Jose.

Steve Wozniak was a very smart boy who was shy around other people. He liked sports, playing Little League and competing on a swim team. Yet he loved electronics.

Encouraged by his father, an engineer, Steve built an amateur radio and studied electronic designs. Then he worked at building simple computing machines. For one that could add and subtract, he won first prize at a science fair.

In high school, Wozniak was a loner. Yet he built a reputation as a prankster. His electronics skills helped. He once put a ticking machine in a gym bag. Thinking it contained a bomb, the principal quickly ran it out to a field. Woz was punished, but he attracted the attention of other students, including Steve Jobs.

Jobs was beginning to show what kind of person he would be as head of a major corporation. When he was thirteen, he called Bill Hewlett of Hewlett-Packard to ask whether he would give him some parts he needed for a device. Hewlett not only gave the gutsy boy the parts, he offered him a summer job.

As Jobs started high school, Wozniak left for the University of Colorado. (He chose it because he first saw snow there.) Yet he did not care for academic life, so he returned to California and took a programming job. In his spare time, he devoured technical journals and designed computers. Jobs started hanging around, just as he did with the engineers when he was young.

In 1971, Jobs and Wozniak heard about the "phone phreak" Captain Crunch, who had built a "blue box" to make free long-distance calls. Wozniak designed an even better box, which he and Jobs built. The project was questionable, but the two maintained that the challenge of hacking was the reward, not the free service. Woz said, "I would get on the phone all night long and try to figure out how I could work my way through the . . . phone system."[3]

Always ready for fun, Wozniak started a Dial-A-Joke service from his home. He also took a good job at Hewlett-Packard and married Alice Robertson. When Homebrew Computer Club started, he joined right away. Homebrew attracted computer hobbyists. Usable personal computers were still a futuristic dream. At club meetings, Wozniak, Jobs, and others got together and talked about the machines.

After high school, Jobs took off for Reed College in Portland, Oregon. He began to explore Eastern religions. With bad grades, he dropped out of school and eventually returned home. After a trip to India to follow a guru, he came back to California and a job at Atari, the video-game company.

Meanwhile, Woz designed a computer to show off at Homebrew meetings. He tried to "do designs that use one less chip than the last guy."[4] Jobs saw a potential business. He wanted to make and sell Wozniak's machines. Like many at Homebrew, he thought computers could change the world, but he also knew they could make money.

The computer Woz built became the Apple, and a company—Apple Computer, Inc.—was born. It was 1976.

Now it was time to get busy and assemble computers. To raise money for parts, Jobs sold his van, and Wozniak sold his calculator. The Jobs family's garage turned into their workplace. When the Byte Shop, a local computer store, ordered fifty units from them, Jobs and Woz were thrilled.

Jobs excelled at planning, talking, and bargaining. He also had self-confidence enough for two. Yet he was smart enough to know they needed help.[5] He hired Mike Markkula, retired from Intel, to be chairman and to help obtain funding for Apple.

Wozniak worked on a new improved Apple. To replace the magnetic tape storage, he designed a floppy disk. He also created slots inside for add-ons. Jobs searched for light plastic cases, more attractive than metal. The Apple II would be the first popular personal computer.[6]

Jobs was not a suit-and-tie person. Often he went barefoot and wore torn jeans, even to meet clients. Still he was intense, bold, and a first-rate salesman.[7]

In early 1977, the company moved from the garage to a real office. Jobs wanted Wozniak full-time at Apple. Woz did not want to leave his secure job at Hewlett-Packard. Yet friends, urged by Jobs, coaxed him to leave, and he did. He did not need to worry. From 1977 to 1982, Apple ruled the personal computer market.[8]

In 1981, IBM, with its first personal computer, bit into Apple's market share. Jobs fought back with the Apple IIe, Lisa (named for his daughter born in 1978), and Macintosh. As the company grew, Jobs cleaned up his look. Yet he did not soften his treatment of employees. He could be blunt, even rude.

Apple tried to regain its lead. A lot of tension built inside the company. Amid a power struggle, Jobs left in 1985.

Wozniak had already left in 1981. He was never interested in the business side of Apple. He said, "I missed tinkering. I just wanted to be an engineer."[9] After he and Alice divorced in 1980, he married Candi Clark, a former Olympic kayaker, in 1981. They had met in a water-gun fight at an Apple lab.

Woz returned to Apple in 1982 to design the Lisa but left again in early 1985. The company had changed; Wozniak and Jobs were no longer friends.

Apple stock made the two Steves millionaires. Wozniak used some of his to host two huge music festivals. He also went back to college, graduating in 1986 from the University of California, Berkeley.

Classic 1980s Apple Mac SE® desktop personal computer with mouse and keyboard

Woz became a devoted family man. He and Candi had three children: Jesse, Sara, and Stephen Gary, Jr. Shortly before their last baby was born, the two divorced. He then married Suzanne Mulkern and taught computers in the public schools. After their divorce in 2004, Woz married Janet Hill in 2008. The next year, he became the chief scientist for Fusion-io, a software and data-storage company near Salt Lake City, Utah.

Jobs, who described himself as "a tool builder,"[10] took his stock money and started NeXT Software, Inc., a computer company. Yet NeXT never took off like Apple. In late 1996, Apple announced that it would buy NeXT and that Jobs would return.

Jobs also bought Pixar, a computer-animation company, from George Lucas of the *Star Wars* movies. For a time, Pixar made commercials and computer-graphics software. Then, in 1995 its first film, *Toy Story*, came out. It was a huge hit. Pixar went on to release many more award-winning animated films, including *Monsters, Inc.* (2001); *Finding Nemo* (2003); *Cars* (2006); and two more *Toy Story* movies.

Jobs lived in Palo Alto. He and his wife, Laurene Powell, whom he married in 1991, had three children: Reed, born in 1991; Erin, in 1995; and Eve, in 1998. At Apple, he oversaw the development of smaller and faster products: the iMac in 1998; the iPod music player in 2001; the iPhone in 2007; and the iPad tablet computer in 2010. He stayed at

Apple until just a few weeks before he died from pancreatic cancer on October 5, 2011. The company was still celebrating the release of the iPhone 4S, which featured a voice-recognition system to operate a virtual assistant called Siri.

"We've lost something we won't get back . . . ," Woz said about his friend's death; "he brought a lot of life to the world."[11]

Jobs and Wozniak took a hobbyist's toy and turned it into a useful tool for the average person. They introduced the mouse, menus, and easy instructions to the public. Woz the designer and Jobs the salesman joined the computer revolution at the right time. Together, they built Apple, setting the standard for user-friendly computers.

9

Marc Hannah

Graphics Master

An alien spaceship hovers over the White House. A cow flies through the air during a tornado. A scientist changes from fat to thin and back again in seconds. Of course, it's not real, but it looks real. It's movie magic!

These special effects thrilled viewers of *Independence Day, Twister*, and *The Nutty Professor*. The scenes or actions may be impossible in real life, but with computer-generated graphics, they can happen. What a director imagines comes alive on the screen.

Marc Hannah designed the computers that make these effects possible. He was one of the cofounders of Silicon Graphics, Inc. This company was the leader in providing computers that

Marc Hannah

produce the "oh, wow!" images that dazzle moviegoers. His systems have equipped users in many industries with powerful graphics tools.

Marc Regis Hannah was born on October 13, 1956, in Chicago. He was the fourth in a family of five, with older brothers, Hubert Jr., and Dwayne; younger brother, Don; and sister, Judy. Both his parents had college degrees, and they raised their children to value education. Hubert, an accountant, and Edith, a teacher, encouraged their son to study hard. His mother, especially, played an active role in her son's education. He did very well in school.

As a young boy, Hannah enjoyed tinkering with mechanical things. He admits he watched a lot of television, but he also read.[1] Except for one year at a private school (as a high school freshman), he attended public schools. His favorite subjects were math and science.[2] When he was a senior in high school, he took a programming course. "That really directed me into computing,"[3] he remembers.

As he prepared for college, Hannah had to decide what to study. Should he major in physics or engineering? He liked both. A Bell Laboratories scholarship in electrical engineering clinched that decision. He entered the Illinois Institute of Technology and graduated in 1977. Another award from Bell Labs sent him to Stanford University in California. There, he earned a master's degree in 1978. In 1985, he received his Ph.D. All of his degrees were in electrical engineering.

Teaching at Stanford at the time was Jim Clark, a professor of engineering. Clark wanted to use computers to manipulate 3-D (three-dimensional) images. He invented the Geometry Engine®, a chip especially for computer graphics. With this chip, the picture on the computer screen would rotate. Then the user could see the image in 3-D.

Hannah explains:

> If you have a picture of a house on paper, . . . you get to see it from just one specific angle, but with 3-D you can use the computer to view that same house from different angles, change the color, raise the roof, change the floor plan, modify sections of it. It gives you the ability to move around like that. It's quicker and easier on computer.[4]

Hannah, looking for an interesting research project, was introduced to Clark. They developed a working chip at Stanford. (Part of Hannah's dissertation was on the Geometry Engine®.) Clark decided to build a company and invited Hannah to help. "You can make yourself a million dollars," Clark said, "and have some fun."[5]

In 1982, Marc Hannah joined Jim Clark and five others to found Silicon Graphics, Inc. They based their company in Mountain View, California. Their business would be the design, building, and sales of high-performance systems. Hannah went to work on the Geometry Engine®. He redesigned it, making it much faster. It would be used in the company's products for the next six years.

As the business grew, it attracted many big-name companies. They found Silicon Graphics products excellent for many functions.

Their workstations provided the high-end graphics. These were just what Hollywood needed for some of its biggest special effects. Visual-effects technicians have used the products that Hannah designed to create stunning scenes. Many scenes would have been impossible, or at least difficult and too costly to produce, just a few years before.

Hannah's job was looking to the future and anticipating what could be designed. "The movie industry is the one that constantly pushes our technology,"[6] Hannah said in 1995. The quest for ever-better effects goes on. Creatures, crowds, stunts, whole new worlds come from products Hannah helped create.

Industrial Light and Magic, George Lucas's company, uses Silicon Graphics products. So does Steven Spielberg's DreamWorks SKG. Many blockbuster movies, such as *Avatar, Pirates of the Caribbean,* and *Titanic*, the *Harry Potter* films, and the *Shrek* movies, feature effects done with Silicon Graphics computers. Music videos and TV commercials have also used the company's technology.

Besides the entertainment industry, business, government, and science also rely on Silicon Graphics products for their computer-graphics needs.

Silicon Graphics workstations are used by engineers who design cars and planes. The Boeing 777, a long-range wide body twin-engine jet, was computer-designed with Silicon Graphics products. In addition to building car and plane bodies, the computers plan the mechanical areas too. An important part of auto-safety study, crash testing, is also done with computers.

In hospitals, imaging done on Silicon Graphics products helps doctors diagnose disease. Biochemists develop new medicines, using molecular modeling—on the computer. Pilots train with flight simulation. Computers help scientists in oil and gas exploration. The scientists can visualize problems and explore solutions.

Besides these large-scale applications, Silicon Graphics, Inc., was making products that would be directly used by consumers. In 1993, the company entered into an agreement with Nintendo to create Nintendo 64®, a video game console, Silicon Graphics was also the power behind some of the early handheld personal organizers and planners. It also made systems and software that businesses would use to build Web sites with 3-D graphics.

While Hannah was busy as vice-president and chief scientist at Silicon Graphics, Inc., he also worked at a number of other ventures. He became one of the owners of Rondeau Bay Construction Company. This minority-owned firm solves technical problems in the building industry. For example, repairs to sewer pipelines in a unique way, Hannah explained, "Rondeau Bay has a technology for going in and actually putting a plastic liner in the interior of the pipeline, so that you don't have

Marc Hannah designed the computers that make the computer graphics in movies like *Shrek* possible. Mike Myers who was the voice of Shrek is shown here.

to tear up the street and dig up the pipeline. It's cheaper and less disruptive."[8]

Hannah was on the technical advisory board of Warp Speed Communications. This company is in the high-speed communications business. He also served on the board of directors of Silicon Magic. It designs fast memory chips and multimedia chips.

He was involved in the traveling museum display, "Black Achievers in Science." He was one of the scientists chosen for this exhibit. Developed by the Museum of Science and Industry in Chicago, it featured photos, models, and hands-on devices. When kids see Hannah and others as role models, they might just consider science as a career.

Hannah is always thinking of the better, the faster, the more affordable. In the 1990s, his goal was to make this computing power available to the average person. "Computers are great things, but right now they are too hard to use,"[9] he said. He thought a lot about designing from the point of view of the user. "One of the most important things is understanding what they want to do. What is the problem they are trying to solve?"[10] Now, because of the advances he made in computer graphics, computers and handheld devices, such as smartphones, have many easy-to-use applications, including mapping

"The end result is a computer that is very flexible. It includes a lot of new features and makes older features faster,"[11] he explained. For his designs, he has earned more than fifteen patents.

Hannah does not actually make an exploding spacecraft for a movie or a sleek new car body. He designs for the people who do these things. In this way, his job is as creative as those who work each day in visual effects.

"I . . . focus on the graphics side of things," he said. He has to decide "what performance level we are targeting, what the features will be and what price range we are seeking."[12]

He most enjoys "seeing how people use our computers, usually at the front end of product design, going out to collect information. People do things we didn't think of. It's fascinating."[13]

Hannah was semiretired from Silicon Graphics, Inc., when a new opportunity came along. Friend Ronald L. Jones asked him to be the chief technology officer at his startup company SongPro. Hannah was thrilled to be able to help his friend, and he enjoyed the challenges of making music and video streaming secure for users.[14]

As a cofounder of the pioneering computer-graphics company, Marc Hannah helped build the reputation of Silicon Graphics, Inc. As an architect of graphics systems, he helped build a safer, healthier, and more entertaining world.

10

Marc Andreessen

Navigator on the Net

Working eighteen hours a day; living on pizza, pop, and every other kind of junk food; writing lines, and lines, and more lines of computer code; talking about everything—for Marc Andreessen [ann–dree–sen], this was life while he and Eric Bina wrote Mosaic. This piece of software made using the Internet much easier.

Andreessen was born in July 1971. He grew up in the small town of New Lisbon, Wisconsin. His father, Lowell, was a seed salesman and is now retired. Patricia, his mother, works at the catalog company Lands' End.

Marc was fascinated by computers from an early age. When he was eight, he learned BASIC (a programming language) from a library book. By

Marc Andreessen

sixth grade, he was a regular at the computer in the school library. He even wrote a program for that computer to do his math assignments. Yet when the janitor turned off the power at the end of the day, the program was erased.[1] Soon he was programming at home, however, when his parents gave him his own computer in seventh grade.

In high school, Andreessen was a good student. Eager to learn, he read books on many subjects. He was also a friendly young man with a sense of humor.[2] When it was time to choose a college, he picked the University of Illinois at Urbana-Champaign. At first he thought he might study electrical engineering.[3] Yet in time, he chose computer science.

Like many college students, he worked and took classes. He was hired by the school's National Center for Supercomputing Applications (NCSA). This famous research center was a great place for a young computer scientist. It was here that Andreessen met like-minded techies. He also surfed the Internet for the first time.

The Internet is a huge network of computers. A user can surf, or travel through, these linked computers to find information, do business, communicate, and have fun.

At the time, though, it was not an easy place to get through. The Internet grew out of Arpanet, which was begun by physicists. Later the World Wide Web started. It was full of tricky commands and brought up only text. Andreessen recalls, " . . . you were still expected to be a rocket scientist to actually access anything."[4]

At NCSA, Andreessen wrote code for programs. At the same time, he was thinking about the Internet. How could he find his way through the maze of information? What software could he write to do this?

In late December 1992, Andreessen and his friend, fellow NCSA employee Eric Bina, were at a café. Andreessen said, "Let's go for it."[5] From January to March of the next year, the two wrote Mosaic. They formed one of those perfect partnerships that happen every so often in the history of computers. Andreessen the visionary and Bina the technical whiz worked together to conquer the Internet.

Their idea was to make traveling the Web easy for anyone. Mosaic did this. Andreessen and Bina built a graphics interface. Users could point at underlined words or pictures and click on them with their mouse. Using hypertext (links to related information), Mosaic would then take them from one site to the next, to the next, and so on. With Mosaic and hypertext, finding a way through the Internet is as easy as "point and click."

Andreessen enlisted other NCSA programmers to work on Mosaic. Now it would run on PCs and Macs. When it was completed, the university put Mosaic on the Internet, where anyone was allowed to download it for free. In a year, over 2 million users did just that.

Andreessen graduated in December 1993. With a bachelor's degree in computer science, he took off for Silicon Valley. There, he found a job with Enterprise Integration Technologies. He wrote software for its Internet security products.

One day in February 1994, he looked at his e-mail and found this note from Jim Clark: "You may not know me, but I'm the founder of Silicon Graphics. . . . I've resigned and intend to form a new company. Would you be interested in getting together to talk?"[6]

Of course, Andreessen met with Clark. For eight weeks, they tossed around ideas. Interactive TV and its software appealed to Clark. Yet Andreessen convinced him that the Internet was the way of the future. They decided to create a Mosaic Killer—an Internet browser that would have even better features than the original Mosaic. Its nickname was "Mozilla."

Andreessen supplied the idea. Clark put up $4 million. Now they were ready to start their company. Based in Mountain View, California, Mosaic Communications began in April 1994. However, the University of Illinois objected to the use of that name. The school said it owned it. It threatened a lawsuit; it was settled out of court. Andreessen and Clark renamed their company Netscape Communications Corporation.

Andreessen brought Eric Bina and his other NCSA Mosaic teammates into the company too. They all worked hard to make their product secure, fast, and able to handle graphics.[7] The browser they created was named Netscape® Navigator.

By December, it was ready to go. Once again, to the delight of Internet users, the browser was put on the Net to be downloaded for free. In just a few months, 70 percent of people browsing the Internet were using Navigator.

For Netscape to make money, however, the company needed other products. Andreessen and his team came up with servers. With a server, a company can build a website on the Net. Its customers can "visit" the site to view its content: publications, photographs, videos, ads.

In January 1995, Jim Barksdale was hired as CEO (chief executive officer). He brought his expertise from running AT&T's cellular division. The three top men were called "Marc, Bark, and Clark."

At Netscape, things were a bit different from some other computer companies. Conference rooms had funny names, such as the Cat in the Hat Room.[8]

Netscape stock was first sold in August 1995. The IPO (initial public offering) was $28 per share of stock. The trading began, however, at $71. Within a few months, it was at $100. This made the early employees who owned stock very rich.

Andreessen kept it in perspective, though. "It's all just play money unless we have a profitable business over the long term,"[9] he observed.

Competition came in August 1996. As expected, Microsoft brought out its browser, Microsoft® Internet Explorer. The next week, Netscape introduced its new version of Navigator. Many magazines played it up as an epic battle. Here was Bill Gates, pushed by Marc Andreessen into recognizing the Internet. It was Microsoft versus Netscape; which browser would win?

Many Net users cheered it as a real choice. Both companies were committed to providing quality upgrades. Information highway travelers could see a bright future ahead.

This increased Net activity built new businesses within the computer industry. Companies and consultants sprang up to help users. New magazines that specialize in the Net started publishing (some online). Conferences, speakers, and books devoted to cruising the Internet exploded onto the scene.

Andreessen believes the field is wide open to anyone: "Today, with a little luck and brains and timing, any kid with a computer can do what Netscape has done."[10]

Marc Andreessen no longer writes programs. On September 9, 1999, he and Ben Horowitz started LoudCloud, an Internet technology company. It eventually became known as Opsware Inc., "the leader in data center automation," and in 2007

Traveling the Internet is easier because of software written by Marc Andreessen.

was bought by HP for $1.6 billion.[11] Since then, he and Horowitz started a venture capital business called Andreessen Horowitz, or A16Z. They invest money in technology startups: They help young companies succeed, and when those companies are sold, A16Z makes a profit. For example, they invested $50 million in Skype, which allows users to talk to and even see one another over the Internet. Two years later, Skype was sold for $8.5 billion—four times their investment.[12] Andreessen is also on the board of directors for several huge Internet companies, including Facebook and eBay.

Even with his fame and fortune, Andreessen lives modestly. Like many computer programmers, he dresses casually and likes pizza and burgers. Not just a computer expert, he has a wide range of knowledge. He can discuss history and philosophy as well as business and technology. He keeps up to date with dozens of newspapers and magazines. He likes classical music. In 2006, he married Laura Arrillaga, a business professor at Stanford University. Together, they started a charity called the Marc and Laura Andreessen Foundation.

Andreessen could see the future when he said in 1995, "I don't see a Netscape-controlled future for the Net. The Internet is too dynamic and innovative. No single company will control everything."[13] In 1998, Internet giant AOL bought Netscape, but the brand still exists. It has become an Internet service provider (ISP) and a social news Web site.

What did Andreessen and his fellow Netscape workers create? Users now easily navigate the Internet. Millions of sites or pages have been built on the Net, with more coming on daily. A company can construct an "intranet"—an internal network for sharing information, using Net browser technology. Companies can sell their products directly from their sites or through links on their sites to other vendors.

With billions of users and millions of potential uses, the Internet grows. Andreessen, through Mosaic and Navigator, gave it the jump start it needed.

Chapter Notes

Chapter 1. Herman Hollerith

1. Marguerite Zientara, *The History of Computing* (Framingham, Mass.: CW Communications, 1981), p. 22.

2. Geoffrey D. Austrian, *Herman Hollerith: Forgotten Giant of Information Processing* (New York: Columbia University, 1982), pp. 2–3.

3. Ibid., p. 6.

4. Keith S. Reid-Green, "The History of Census Tabulation," *Scientific American*, February 1989, p. 98.

5. Austrian, pp. 39–40.

6. F. W. Kistermann, "The Invention and Development of the Hollerith Punched Card," *Annals of the History of Computing*, 1991, p. 252.

7. Reid-Green, p. 101.

8. Austrian, p. 69.

9. Ibid., p. 107.

10. Ibid., p. 76.

11. Ibid., p. 88.

12. Ibid., p. 182.

13. Ibid., p. 181.

14. Ibid., p. 211.

Chapter 2. John von Neumann

1. William Poundstone, *Prisoner's Dilemma: Von Neumann, Game Theory, and the Puzzle of the Bomb* (New York: Doubleday, 1992), p. 12.

2. Ibid., p. 13.

3. Norman Macrae, *John von Neumann* (New York: Pantheon, 1992), pp. 47–48.

4. Ibid., pp. 7–8.

5. Poundstone, p. 17.

6. Ibid., p. 25.

7. Herman H. Goldstine, *The Computer From Pascal to von Neumann* (Princeton, N.J.: Princeton University, 1972), p. 171.

8. David Ritchie, *The Computer Pioneers* (New York: Simon and Schuster, 1986), p. 169.

9. Macrae, p. 275.

10. Stan Augarten, *Bit by Bit: An Illustrated History of Computers* (New York: Ticknor and Fields, 1984), p. 137.

11. William Aspray, *John von Neumann and the Origins of Modern Computing* (Cambridge, Mass.: MIT, 1990), p. xv.

12. Poundstone, p. 39.

13. Klara von Neumann, Preface in *The Computer and the Brain* by John von Neumann (New Haven, Conn.: Yale University, 1958), pp. v–vi.

Chapter 3. Grace Hopper

1. Marguerite Zientara, *The History of Computing* (Framingham, Mass.: CW Communications, 1981), p. 52.

2. Ibid., p. 51.

3. George Leopold, "Beacon for the Future," *Datamation*, October 1, 1986, p. 109.

4. Lynn Gilbert and Gaylen Moore, *Particular Passions: Talks With Women Who Have Shaped Our Times* (New York: Clarkson N. Potter, 1981), p. 59.

5. Leopold, pp. 109–110.

6. Verne G. Kopytoff, "Japanese 'K' Computer Is Ranked Most Powerful," *New York Times*, June 19, 2011, <http://www.nytimes.com/2011/06/20/technology/20computer.html?_r=1> (accessed April 27, 2012).

7. Janet Fiderio, "Grace Hopper: First Lady of Programming," *Computerworld*, November 3, 1986, p. 143.

8. Eileen Keerdoja, "'The Grand Old Lady of Software,'" *Newsweek*, May 9, 1983, p. 13H.

9. Fiderio, p. 143.

10. "Grace Hopper, 85, Dead; Was Software Pioneer," *Electronic News*, January 6, 1992, p. 8.

11. Corey Sandler, "Keeping Up With Grace," *PC Magazine*, December 1983, p. 204.

12. Leopold, p. 110.

13. Gilbert, p. 62.

Chapter 4. John W. Mauchly and J. Presper Eckert, Jr.

1. Robert Slater, *Portraits in Silicon* (Cambridge, Mass.: MIT, 1987), p. 66.

2. Marguerite Zientara, *The History of Computing* (Framingham, Mass.: CW Communications, 1981), p. 49.

3. Slater, p. 68.

4. Ibid.

5. Ibid.

6. John W. Mauchly, "The ENIAC," in *A History of Computing in the Twentieth Century* (New York: Academic, 1980), p. 543.

7. Philip Elmer-DeWitt, "A Birthday Party for ENIAC," *Time*, February 24, 1986, p. 63.

8. "Presper Eckert Interview," in *Development of the ENIAC Interviews, Smithsonian Videohistory Collection, Record Unit 9537*, February 2, 1988. Internet site <http://www.si.edu/resource/tours/comphist/eckert.htm>(April 29, 2012).

9. George Harrar, "In the Beginning . . . " (interview with J. Presper Eckert), *Computerworld*, November 3, 1986, p. 6 (special section).

10. Slater, p. 77.

11. Nancy Stern, *From ENIAC to UNIVAC* (Bedford, Mass.: Digital, 1981), p. 12.

12. "Thanks for the Memories," *Datamation*, September 1982, p. 32.

Chapter 5. An Wang

1. An Wang, *Lessons: An Autobiography* (Reading, Mass.: Addison-Wesley, 1986), p. 21.

2. Ibid., p. 27.

3. Ibid., p. 73.

4. "Dr. An Wang: The Renaissance Man of Office Systems," *Sales & Marketing Management*, January 18, 1982, p. 19.

5. Karen Berney, "An Wang: Getting to the Essentials," *Nation's Business*, December 1987, p. 86.

6. Wang, p. 155.

7. Berney, p. 85.

8. Wang, p. 237.

9. James Connolly, "An Wang Says Entrepreneurial Road Has Become Tougher," *Computerworld*, November 3, 1986, p. 108.

10. Laura B. Smith, "In a Word: Service," *PC Week*, June 3, 1996, p. A8.

11. Wang, p. 214.

12. Ibid., p. 239.

Chapter 6. Jack Kilby and Robert Noyce

1. Phone interview with Jack Kilby, December 3, 1996.

2. T. R. Reid, *The Chip: How Two Americans Invented the Microchip and Launched a Revolution* (New York: Simon and Schuster, 1984), p. 55.

3. Samuel C. Florman, "Anonymous Heroes," *Technology Review*, January 1988, p. 20.

4. Reid, second page in picture section following p. 64.

5. Ibid., p. 12.

6. Ibid., p. 78.

7. Ibid., p. 95.

8. Phone interview with Jack Kilby, December 3, 1996.

9. Ibid.

10. Walter Guzzardi, "The U.S. Business Hall of Fame," *Fortune*, March 13, 1989, p. 132.

11. Michael R. Leibowitz, "Founding Father," *PC Computing*, May 1989, p. 100.

12. "The Nobel Prize in Physics 2000: Zhores I. Alferov, Herbert Kroemer, Jack S. Kilby," <http://www.nobelprize.org/nobel_prizes/physics/laureates/2000/index.html> (April 29, 2012).

Chapter 7. Bill Gates

1. Stephen Manes and Paul Andrews, *Gates* (New York: Doubleday, 1993), p. 19.

2. Ibid., p. 24.

3. Michael A. Cusumano and Richard W. Selby, *Microsoft Secrets* (New York: Free Press, 1995), p. 23.

4. Bill Gates, *The Road Ahead* (New York: Viking, 1995), p. 1.

5. "Bill Gates & Paul Allen Talk," *Fortune*, October 2, 1995, p. 70.

6. Manes, p. 58.

7. Paul Freiberger and Michael Swaine, *Fire in the Valley: The Making of the Personal Computer* (Berkeley, Calif.: Osborne/McGraw-Hill, 1984), p. 141.

8. Gates, p. xi.

9. "Bill Gates & Paul Allen Talk," p. 70.

10. Ibid., p. 24.

11. Daniel Ichbiah and Susan L. Knepper, *The Making of Microsoft* (Rocklin, Calif.: Prima, 1991), p. 39.

12. Gates, p. 4.

13. Ibid., p. 225.

14. "Bill and Melinda Gates Give 95% of Wealth to Charity," *BBC News*, October 18, 2010, <http://www.bbc.co.uk/news/entertainment-arts-11565953>(April 29, 2012).

15. David Hayes, "In the Future, Computers Will Talk," *Kansas City Star*, November 20, 1996, p. B-1.

Chapter 8. Steven Jobs and Stephen Wozniak

1. Jeffrey S. Young, *Steve Jobs: The Journey Is the Reward* (Glenview, Ill.: Scott, Foresman, 1988), p. 21.

2. Ibid., p. 23.

3. Tom Morganthau, "A Wizard Called 'Woz,'" *Newsweek*, September 20, 1982, p. 69.

4. Steven Levy, *Hackers: Heroes of the Computer Revolution* (Garden City, N.Y.: Anchor/Doubleday, 1984), p. 248.

5. Ibid., p. 253.

6. Randall E. Stross, *Steve Jobs and the NeXT Big Thing* (New York: Atheneum, 1993), p. 8.

7. Young, p. 100.

8. Robert Slater, *Portraits in Silicon* (Cambridge, Mass.: MIT, 1987), p. 315.

9. Chet Flippo, "Once an Electronics Nerd," *People*, May 30, 1983, p. 95.

10. Jeff Goodell, "Looking for the Next Revolution: The *Rolling Stone* Interview With Steve Jobs," *Rolling Stone*, June 16, 1994, p. 102.

11. Rachel Metz, "Steve Wozniak on Steve Jobs's Death: 'We've Lost Something We Won't Get Back,'" *The Huffington Post*, October 6, 2011; <http://www.huffingtonpost.com/2011/10/06/steve-wozniak-steve-jobs-death_n_997533.html> (May 8, 2012).

Chapter 9. Marc Hannah

1. Phone interview with Marc Hannah, March 7, 1997.

2. Ibid.

3. Ibid.

4. "Marc Hannah: Special Effects Wiz," *Ebony*, February 1993, p. 57.

5. Sonya Stinson, "Computer Architect Builds Success in 3-D," *Black Collegian*, October 1995, pp. 96+.

6. Ibid.

7. Phone interview with Marc Hannah, March 7, 1997.

8. Stinson, pp. 96+.

9. Phone interview with Marc Hannah, March 7, 1997.

10. Ibid.

11. Ibid.

12. "Marc Hannah: Special Effects Wiz," p. 56.

13. Phone interview with Marc Hannah, March 7, 1997.

14. Jill Yesko, "SongPro CTO Marc Hannah: Silicon Valley's Master Designer," *Blackengineer.com*, April 15, 2003; <http://www.blackengineer.com/artman/publish/printer_55.shtml> (May 7, 2012).

Chapter 10. Marc Andreessen

1. Rick Tetzeli, "What It's Really Like to Be Marc Andreessen," *Fortune*, December 9, 1996, p. 142.

2. Ibid.

3. Albert G. Holzinger, "Netscape Founder Points, and It Clicks," *Nation's Business*, January 1996, p. 32.

4. Ibid.

5. George Gilder, "The Coming Software Shift," *Forbes ASAP*, August 28, 1995, p. 154.

6. David A. Kaplan, "Nothing but Net," *Newsweek*, December 25, 1995/January 1, 1996, p. 35.

7. Alison L. Sprout, "The Rise of Netscape," *Fortune*, July 10, 1995, p. 141.

8. Joshua Cooper Ramo, "Winner Take All," *Time*, September 16, 1996, p. 62.

9. Chip Bayers, "Why Bill Gates Wants to Be the Next Marc Andreessen," *Wired*, December 1995, p. 236.

10. Jeff Goodell, "After the Gold Rush," *Rolling Stone*, May 1, 1997, p. 65.

11. HP Press Release, "HP Closes Opsware Acquisition: Deal Adds Data Center Automation to HP Business Technology Optimization Software Portfolio," September 21, 2007 <http://www.hp.com/hpinfo/newsroom/press/2007/070921xa.html?jumpid=reg_R1002_USEN> (May 8, 2012).

12. Connie Guglielmo and Tomio Geron, "Andreessen, Horowitz: Venture Capital's New Bad Boys," *Forbes*, May 21, 2012; <http://www.forbes.com/sites/connieguglielmo/2012/05/02/andreessen-horowitz-venture-capitals-new-bad-boys/> (May 8, 2012).

13. Bayers, p. 236.

Further Reading

Aronson, Marc. *Bill Gates: A Twentieth-Century Life*. New York, N.Y.: Viking, 2009.

Brashares, Ann. *Steve Jobs: Think Different*. Brookfield, Conn.: Twenty-First Century Books, 2001.

Byman, Jeremy. *Andrew Grove and the Intel Corporation*. Greensboro, N.C.: Morgan Reynolds, 1999.

Cleveland, Donald B. *Seven Wonders of Communication*. Minneapolis, Minn.: Twenty-First Century Books, 2010.

Hart-Davis, Adam, ed. *Science: The Definitive Visual Guide*. New York, N.Y.: DK Pub., 2009.

Haven, Kendall F. and Donna Clark. *100 Most Popular Scientists for Young Adults: Biographical Sketches and Professional Paths*. Englewood, Colo.: Libraries Unlimited, 1999.

Mattern, Joanne. *Grace Hopper: Computer Pioneer*. New York: Powerkids Press, 2003.

Otfinoski, Steven. *Computers*. New York: Marshall Cavendish Benchmark, 2008.

Pollack, Pam and Meg Belviso. *Who Was Steve Jobs?* New York: Grosset and Dunlap, 2012.

Reid, T. R. *The Chip: How Two Americans Invented the Microchip and Launched a Revolution*. New York: Random House, 2001.

Tomecek, Stephen M. *What a Great Idea: Inventions That Changed the World*. New York: Scholastic Nonfiction, 2003.

Tracy, Kathleen. *Marc Andreessen and the Development of the Web Browser*. Bear, Del.: Mitchell Lane, 2002.

Internet Addresses

Open Directory—Kids and Teens: People and Society: Biography

Find out more about the lives of the computer scientists by visiting this site:

<http://www.dmoz.org/Kids_and_Teens/People_and_Society/Biography/>

Then click on *Computer Scientists.*

PBS: A Science Odyssey—People and Discoveries

To find out more the inventions and the inventors from the wireless to the World Wide Web, visit this site:

<http://www.pbs.org/wgbh/aso/databank/> Then click on *Technology.*

Index